I Can Read!

First
READING

Biscuit
and the
Big Parade!

story by Alyssa Satin Capucilli
pictures by Pat Schories

HARPER
An Imprint of HarperCollinsPublishers

Dear Parent:
Your child's love of reading starts here!

Every child learns to read in a different way and at his or her own speed. Some go back and forth between reading levels and read favorite books again and again. Others read through each level in order. You can help your young reader improve and become more confident by encouraging his or her own interests and abilities. From books your child reads with you to the first books he or she reads alone, there are I Can Read Books for every stage of reading:

SHARED READING
Basic language, word repetition, and whimsical illustrations, ideal for sharing with your emergent reader

BEGINNING READING
Short sentences, familiar words, and simple concepts for children eager to read on their own

READING WITH HELP
Engaging stories, longer sentences, and language play for developing readers

READING ALONE
Complex plots, challenging vocabulary, and high-interest topics for the independent reader

ADVANCED READING
Short paragraphs, chapters, and exciting themes for the perfect bridge to chapter books

I Can Read Books have introduced children to the joy of reading since 1957. Featuring award-winning authors and illustrators and a fabulous cast of beloved characters, I Can Read Books set the standard for beginning readers.

A lifetime of discovery begins with the magical words "I Can Read!"

Visit www.icanread.com for information
on enriching your child's reading experience.

For my newest paraders—Stella Hazel,
Dylan Lazarus, Rae Samantha,
Ezra Dylan, and Logan Sam!
—A.S.C.

I Can Read Book® is a trademark of HarperCollins Publishers.

Biscuit and the Big Parade! Text copyright © 2018 by Alyssa Satin Capucilli Illustrations copyright © 2018 by Pat Schories All rights reserved. Manufactured in U.S.A. No part of this book may be used or reproduced in any manner whatsoever without written permission except in the case of brief quotations embodied in critical articles and reviews. For information address HarperCollins Children's Books, a division of HarperCollins Publishers, 195 Broadway, New York, NY 10007.
www.icanread.com

ISBN 978-0-06-243615-3 (trade bdg.)—ISBN 978-0-06-243614-6 (pbk.)

Library of Congress Control Number: 2017932867

18 19 20   LSCC   10 9 8 7 6 5 4 3 2   ❖   First Edition

It's time for the big parade,
Biscuit.
Woof, woof!

Let's find a good spot,
Biscuit.

There will be so much to see.

Woof, woof!

Rum-pa-pa-pum!
Rum-pa-pa-pum!

Woof, woof!

Hooray!

Here comes the parade!

Woof!

Silly puppy!

No tugging now.

You can't march
in the big parade.
Woof, woof!

Beep! Beep!

Here comes the fire truck,

Biscuit.

Woof!

Ruff!
And you found
the firefighters' dog.
Woof, woof!

Look, Biscuit.

There are jugglers and ponies.

There are big floats, too.

Woof, woof!

Stay here now, Biscuit.
You can't march
in the big parade.
Woof!

Honk! Honk!

Woof!

Funny puppy!

The clowns
are just saying hello.
Woof, woof!

Honk! Honk! Honk! Honk!
Whoosh!

Oh no, Biscuit!

There go the balloons.

What will the clowns do now?

Woof!

Biscuit! Come back.

You can't march
in the big parade.
Woof, woof!

Oh, Biscuit.
You did it.

You caught the balloons!

Woof, woof!

Wait, Biscuit!

Where are you going now?

Woof!

What a good puppy!
It's fun to watch
a big parade.

But it's even more fun
to march along!
Woof!

Rum-pa-pa-pum!

Rum-pa-pa-pum!

Woof, woof!